D0183351

Based on the episode "Chores" by Jon Foster and James Lamont

Adapted by Lauren Holowaty

First published in Great Britain by
HarperCollins *Children's Books* in 2020
HarperCollins *Children's Books* is a division of HarperCollins*Publishers* Ltd,
HarperCollins Publishers
1 London Bridge Street
London SE1 9GF

1 3 5 7 9 10 8 6 4 2

ISBN: 978–0–00–836794–7

Printed in China

Based on the Paddington novels written and created by Michael Bond

PADDINGTON™ and PADDINGTON BEAR™ © Paddington and Company/STUDIOCANAL S.A.S. 2020
Paddington Bear™ and Paddington™ and PB™ are trademarks of Paddington and Company Limited
Licensed on behalf of STUDIOCANAL S.A.S. by Copyrights Group

MIX
Paper from
responsible sources
FSC® C007454

FSC
www.fsc.org

The Adventures of Paddington

The Wrong List

HarperCollins *Children's Books*

Dear Aunt Lucy,

Something most peculiar
happened to me today. In fact,
it seems like things always
happen to me. I'm just that kind
of bear. I was having afternoon
tea with the Browns . . .

Mr Brown came in carrying a tray of freshly baked scones.

"Who wants jam and who wants cream?"

"Both, please!" shouted Jonathan and Judy.

"Mr Brown," began Paddington, who was always incredibly polite, "allow me to help you . . ."

Paddington whisked the tray away from Mr Brown,
sending the scones flying, and the bowl of fluffy cream
spinning through the air . . .

SPLAT!

It landed **smack**
in Mr Brown's face!

"Oh, dear. Let me get that," said Paddington, trying to **lick** the cream off. "We mustn't waste it."

"**Ugh!**" cried Mr Brown. "No, it's all right . . . I'll get a cloth from the kitchen."

"Sorry," said Paddington, thinking what else he could do. "Perhaps I could come and help you with the washing-up?"

In the kitchen, Paddington knocked a teapot off the
table by accident!

"Ahh! I really **don't need** any help, Paddington,"
Mr Brown said, diving to catch it **before it smashed.**
"Washing-up is **my** chore."

"What's a chore?"

"Everyone in the family has a chores list on the fridge," explained Mrs Brown. "Chores are jobs, like doing the laundry or cleaning."

"How exciting! I can't wait to read my chores list!" said Paddington.

"Don't be silly, Paddington! *You* don't need to do family chores," laughed Mr Brown.

The young bear looked sad.

"Oh, I thought I *was* part of the family," he sighed, wandering off.

Mr and Mrs Brown hadn't meant to upset Paddington.
They called an emergency family meeting and wrote
a chores list just for him. It had **one** thing on it –
"Make marmalade".

But, when Mr Brown went
to tell Paddington that he had
his very own list, it fell off the fridge!

That night, Paddington could barely **sleep for excitement.** *A day doing chores from my very own list,* he thought. *It's a* **dream** *come true!*

The next morning, he grabbed the first chores list he saw on the fridge.

"**Clean the bicycle,**" he read aloud. "Sounds **very** important!"

Paddington took Mr Brown's bicycle apart, put it in the bath and gave it a thoroughly good clean with a **toothbrush.**

SCRUB! SCRUB! SCRUB!

When the bicycle was spotless, Paddington put it back together.
He couldn't remember where some bits went, but they were only
small, so he couldn't imagine they were that important.

Later, Mr Brown came running
out of the house, late for work.
He got on his bicycle and . . .

PING! BOING!
BANG! CRASH!
"AARGH!"

Next on the list was: "Polish the floorboards". Paddington thought there was **rather a lot of floor**. Surely that meant it needed **rather a lot of polish?** So he squeezed slick, oily polish all over the floor and began . . .

. . . skating, sliding, slipping

and – "WHOAAA!" – falling over!

The next chore on the list simply said: "Milk". Paddington wasn't sure what that meant, so he drank **all** the milk.

GLUG! GLUG! GLUG!

Then he headed upstairs to do the final chore: "Wallpaper the spare room". *That sounds easier,* he thought, grabbing a wallpaper brush.

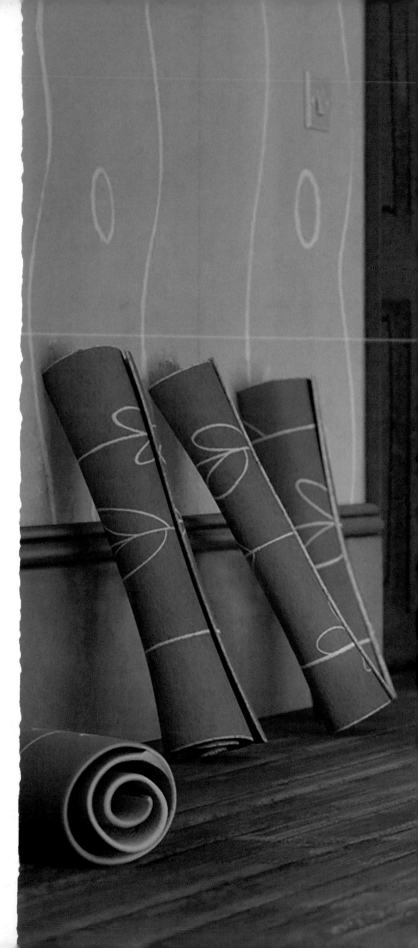

As soon as the Browns came home, they stepped on to the highly polished floor and –

"WHOAAA!"

– slid into an **enormous family pile-up!**

"Whose chore was it to polish the floor?" asked Mrs Bird.

Before anyone could answer, they heard a loud CLATTER and rushed upstairs to find . . .

... Paddington wallpapered to the wall!

"It was the last thing on my chores list," he mumbled.

"Oh, you must've taken *my* list by mistake!" said Mr Brown.

Paddington explained he just wanted to be part of the family.

"You were *always* part of the family, Paddington," said Mrs Brown. "You don't have to do chores to prove that."

Mr Brown helped Paddington down when Judy gasped,
"Look!" and pointed at a drawing behind the
peeling wallpaper.

"You and Jonathan drew that years ago," said Mrs Brown.
"It's a picture of the whole family."
"No, it isn't," said Mr Brown, picking up a pencil . . .

"There," Mr Brown said, adding in a sketch of Paddington. "*Now* it's the whole family!"

The Browns thought the drawing was **absolutely perfect** and decided to **never** wallpaper the room again!

It seems there are an awful lot of chores in the world,
Aunt Lucy. But being part of a family isn't one of them.
Love from,
Paddington